DADDY, HOW DO PLANES FLY?

Daddy, How Do Planes Fly?

by Chris Ryan Miller

ISBN 978-1-257-99175-4

Daddy, how do planes fly?

Planes are able to fly because of their big wings, powerful engines, horizontal tail, vertical tail, and pilots.

The shape of a plane's wings generates LIFT. It's the same as if I were to LIFT you up into the air.

The direction and speed of the airflow creates LIFT on the wings.

The engines provide THRUST. Thrust pushes the airplane forward through the sky. The THRUST helps to LIFT the wings.

This is the VERTICAL tail.

The rudder on the VERTICAL tail points the nose of the airplane left and right. The left and right motion is called YAW.

This is the HORIZONTAL tail.

The HORIZONTAL tail points the nose of the airplane up and down. The up and down motion is called PITCH.

Together the vertical and horizontal tails make up the EMPENNAGE.

The AILERONS on the wings rotate the plane over.

The rotating motion is called ROLL.

With instrumentation pilots control the wings and engines as well as the horizontal and vertical tails.

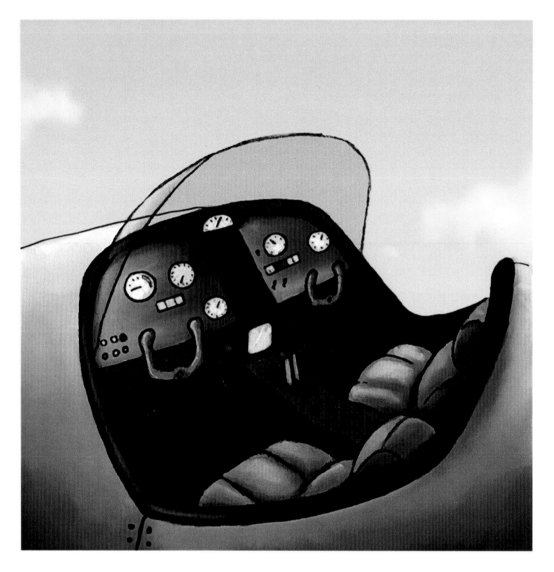

The buttons and switches in front of the PILOTS make up the INSTRUMENTATION.

The pilots use the INSTRUMENTATION to guide the plane through the sky. Pilots get us where we need to go!

Who can be pilots?

Both boys and girls can become pilots and fly airplanes. YOU could be a pilot.

Daddy, now we know how planes fly!